# A Funny Thing Happened

## PAUL LYALLS

Cover illustration and design by Joseph Witchall

D1335306

ISBN : 978-1-9997749-3-6

First published in 2019
by Caboodle Books

A Catalogue record for this book is available from the British Library.
Page Layout by Highlight Type Bureau Ltd, Bradford
Printed and bound by CPI Group (UK) Ltd, Croydon, CR0 4YY

The paper and board used in this book are natural recyclable products made from wood grown in sustainable forests.  The manufacturing processes conform to the environmental regulations of the country of origin.

Caboodle Books Ltd.
Riversdale, 8 Rivock Avenue,
Steeton,  BD20 6SA, UK.

# Introduction

Paul Lyalls is a tall poet with hair that stands up on his head. He writes about things you can see, about the things you can hear and about the things people say. I think that's a Good Thing. One of the strange things about the world around us is that we sometimes forget to notice it. Paul makes you notice it. His poems say, 'Hang on a moment, come over here and look at this; come over here and listen to this.' Then, next time you're awake something in one of Paul's poems will pop up into your head and you'll notice something in the world that you hadn't noticed before. That's a kind of magic - not real magic - the kind of magic that conjurors do: all worked out with secret levers and lids. Paul Lyalls is a tall poet with hair that stands up on his head

Michael Rosen

*Paul and Michael after sharing the stage together at the Edinburgh book festival*

For Joan, Cordelia, Honor and Suria
For little Ezra
Also Ashley, Ann & family & Tiger Alf!
To Luis & family

# Contents

# A Poem Talks

I'm a poem, I'm speaking to you - it's true.
I'm a poem that doesn't know where it's going,
I go this way and that,
I say what I say.
I can say anything.
On a piece of paper I may be flat,
but when you read me
I fill your mind
with people, places, ideas of every kind.
I'm a poem that doesn't know where it's going,
on a river of description I'm flowing
I've got the words doing the rowing.
Words worth knowing. (- Wordsworth knowing!)
Words that go this way and that,
words that move like an acrobat,
in the sails of your imagination blowing.
Because, I'm a poem
that doesn't know where it's going.
But I'm going to make your heart, mind and soul react,
just like they'd do on a roller-coaster
that's reached the top of the track,
not going forwards not going back,
a little piece of knowing that bridges a gap.
I'm a poem that doesn't know where it's going
but I'm going to make a mark.
I write with my heart, I was born in a spark.

I write with my eyes, I write about truth and lies.
I say what I say, I'm words at play
an idea on display that's going to lead
your imagination astray.
Down a pathway with an audible view.
I'm a poem, I'm speaking to you - it's true.

# Hands Up

Hands up all those people who have
ever done anything.
Hands up all those people who have
ever been anywhere.
Hands up all those people
who live in a house or a flat with other people.
Hands up all those people
who have got their own socks.
Hands up all those people
who are really lucky and fortunate in this life and
have two pairs of socks.
Hands up all those people
who think it would be great
if they had an eye on the end of their finger.
Hands up all those people who know
where the sky is.
Hands up all those people who like
putting up their hands.
Hands up all those people
who have annoying little brothers and sisters.
Hands up all those people
who have annoying big brothers and sisters.
Hands up all those people
who ARE an annoying brother or sister.
Hands up all those people who think it would
be a great idea
if there was one special day of the year
when everybody
celebrated their belly buttons
- National Belly Button Day!

# Sleeping Beauty

Sleeping Beauty liked to sleep
at night and in the morning.
She could sleep through anything!
A rainstorm with thunder,
a parrot on her head,
everyone else in the castle snoring,
twenty crying babies,
and even the bed exploding!
Yet she was woken by a kiss,
how possible is this?
Was it because she thought it was true *lurve?*
No, she thought it was a spider on her cheek!

# Church Sign

As I walked along
I passed a church sign.
It said,
'Jumble Sale, this Sunday
- admission 50p.'
Below it was another sign that said,
'Jesus is coming.'
And I thought . . .
they should be charging more than 50p,
that is one very special guest!

# Ask The Audience? Phone A Friend?
## Go Fifty-Fifty
## Or Listen To Your Heart

And then she asks
the Holy Grail of all female questions:
'What are you thinking?'
'Then I want to stare into your eyes forever'
'Ahh, were you really thinking that?'
More importantly, I'm thinking
what should I be thinking?
I'm thinking that I should have thought about you more.
I'm thinking that
if we had our time again,
there's a thousand things I'd do differently.
But what I'm *really* thinking is,
that the next time we go to IKEA
wouldn't it be great
if I were to get inside one of the display wardrobes,
stay silent, hide and wait...
until someone opens the doors,
then leap out
and say, 'What country is this?'
But I know that at this moment
I shouldn't be thinking this.

So instead I say, 'I'm thinking
that if a thousand years
is just a blink in time
then maybe we can gaze into each other's eyes forever.'
And she says, 'Wow, were you thinking that'?
And I say, 'Kind of.'
Then she kisses me, smiles, gazes into my eyes
and says, 'Let's go to IKEA!'

# Grains of Sand

Grains of sand in my hand,
do you understand?
Do you have a plan
to form a sand gang
and build a castle?
Or is it too much hassle?

Grains of sand in my hand,
do you fall in love?
Do you like to mingle,
and do all that cuddly kissy stuff?
Or do you prefer to stay
young free and shingle?

Grains of sand in my hand,
do you wonder,
about the universe,
the meaning of life
and all the things
that are out of reach?
Or do you just lie back
and think life's a beach?

# Ice Age Rhino

Ice age Rhino,
where have you been?
It's been fifty-thousand years
since you've last been seen.
Lost to the world,
dug up by a little girl.
You're no longer the size of a bus,
time has reduced you to a bone
hidden in the dirt and dust.
But, even though you were worn and muddy,
the little girl gave you a tea party.
You sat between a doll and a Tele-tubby.
There was a lot to talk about.
The weather – well the ice has gone.
Nature – yes, the forests are no more
and the glaciers have moved on.
Great beasts no longer roam the land,
everything is built up and well planned.
Dinosaurs only live on in museums and
little children's minds ...
and also in tea parties and the bones they find.

# Maths + % - £ = :(

Somebody take away all the maths
snap all the rulers,
cut the number lines
make a sandwich out of the equal signs
make life better for the go-to-schoolers!
Saw the legs off the times-table
attack the fractions,
exterminate the subtractions
and put long division in prison.
If a child has £5 how many 20p's is that?
Who cares!
If a child has £5
she spends it on a book and sweets
which she shares with her friends,
She doesn't want to carry around
a pocketful of twenty-pence-coins
clanking like a ghost through town.
Maths, nobody loves you.
Maths, nobody will marry you.
Maths, you'll never get a birthday card,
it's your own fault for being too hard!

# Wanting To Want To Be

The puddle wants to be a lake.
The torch wants to be a star.
The match wants to be a forest fire.
The breath wants to be the wind.
The pebble wants to be a mountain.
The jumpers for goalposts want to be Wembley.
The squeak wants to be a roar.
The leaf wants to be a forest.
The dust wants to be a desert.
The scratch wants to be a canyon.
The splash wants to be a wave.
The raindrop wants to be a chandelier.
The word wants to be a poem.
**The last line wants to be the beginning.**

# Belly Button Fluff

Belly button fluff, belly button fluff.
Just what is that belly button stuff?

Always soft, never rough
never much, just enough
to fill your belly button.

Belly button fluff, belly button fluff.
Just what is that belly button stuff?

Like a little belly nest
for tiny belly birds to rest
hidden on your tummy under your vest.

Belly button fluff, belly button fluff.
Just what is that belly button  stuff?

You take it out,
but who puts it in?
And what's it exactly doing?

Belly button fluff, belly button fluff.
Just what is that belly button  stuff?

Why there? Why anywhere?
And why is there never any fluff
in your underwear?

Belly button fluff, belly button fluff.        (whispered)
Just what is that belly button stuff?

# You Want The Tooth,
# You Can't Handle The Tooth

I had my first loose tooth.
It had been annoying me for weeks.
To begin with it had been
a wonderful wobbling miracle,
a miniature seesaw inside my mouth.
My loose tooth was a sign of how cool I was.
My loose tooth was proof that I was now a man
- even though I was only 5 years old.
All the girls couldn't resist my loose tooth.
I'd walk into the school playground
waggling my tooth in their direction.
They'd start screaming and run towards me
all wanting to see my tooth.
Wanting to waggle it.
My tooth was like 'One Direction'
-  except only better,
it could move in *any* direction.
But now I couldn't wait,
I wanted that tooth out
It was the can't wait you get
the night before Christmas.
The can't wait you feel
just before the summer holidays.
The can't wait you have
when a class-mate tells you a secret
and makes you swear never to tell it to anyone

- then you tell
the first person that you see.
I'd heard about the door handle trick.
Not the one when you juggle door handles.
Not the one when you see how many door handles
you can fit inside your mouth.
Nor, the one where you remove all the door
handles from your mum and dad's house
and turn to them and say, 'Can you handle it?'
It's the one where you tie string to a door handle
and the other end to your tooth ...
But, my dad had always said,
'If there is one thing I never want to happen
in our house, it's the door handle trick!'
But, my dad was at work
and the string was in my hand,
and the house was full of door handles
- there was one on every door.
And in my mouth was a wobbly tooth,
that soon would wobble no more.

# The Things Your Parents Tell You

Sometimes it's out of love,
sometimes it's to make you good.
On occasion,
it's a form of cunning persuasion.
And then again, it might just be
that parents have a wild imagination.
I remember seeing my sister cry,
and when I asked why she said, mum had said,
that my sister used to be a fairy that could fly
- but, then my sister said bad things
and the queen of the fairies removed her wings.
They will tell you amazing lies
things that just can't be true.'If you're naughty I'll know,
because every pigeon is watching you, and what they
see, they tell me.'
To make you eat your dinner,
they tell you burnt toast makes you a good singer
and if you eat enough you'll be an X Factor winner.
That 'eating cabbage stops your socks from smelling,
and eating the bread crust will mean your eyes don't
rust.'
'If you poke your belly button too much
your bottom will fall off.'
They'll tell you anything to fill you with sorrow.
'If you eat two bowls of cereal
it means you've eaten two breakfasts,
and it won't be today it'll be tomorrow!'

'If you walk around with your shoelaces undone
hair will start to grow between your toes,
- and also out of your nose.'
But, forgive them, because all of this
is just to help you grow.
And, as we all get older we know
the truth is where it's at.
But, every now and then
I still find my sister checking to see
if her wings have grown back!

# Halloween

On Halloween
my mummy dressed me as a mummy.
She put my pyjamas on,
and wrapped me with rolls and rolls
of white toilet paper until I was fully wrapped.
Until, my mummy had made me into a mummy.
Out I went, knocking on neighbour's doors.
Yelling in a scary voice,
'Something yummy for the mummy,
or else I'll do something you won't find funny!'
Then, it started to rain and I started to unwrap.
The toilet paper started to get soggy,
and to dissolve and turn into paper mash.
Until, I was just this weird looking kid
standing in the rain.
Wearing my pyjamas and wellington boots
with a runny toilet paper face.
A walking toilet paper waterfall.
Then other kids really got scared.
'Ahhh there's a tissue paper monster down our street!'
So I told them,
'My name is Lou Roll
and I'm coming to flush you away.

# Heaven

As I walk across the school playground
a five year old boy runs up to me.
He points two of his fingers at me
and yells 'Bang bang, you're dead!'
I shut my eyes, hold my hands to my heart
and fall to the ground - *in slow motion!*
The five year old boy blows on his fingers
and gallops away on an invisible horse.
I lay there, waiting for the terrible pain of dying to come
but, instead of the agony of death
I hear lots of children laughing.
I open my eyes and see children playing chase and 'It'
as happy as sandwiches in a sandpit.
The birds are singing,
frost and ice recline on the branches of the bare trees.
A brilliant orange sun is in love with a perfect winter blue
sky.
I think to myself, I must be in heaven.
Then an angel is walking towards me.
She speaks softly to me,
telling me that she is a playground assistant,
and can she take me to the staffroom?
And, I think, 'Wow, heaven has a staffroom!'
And I get up off the floor and follow, looking for her
wings.

Inside the staffroom, heaven gets even better.
The angel makes me tea, in a clean cup,
and offers me chocolate biscuits ...
and that's when I realise that it ***must*** be heaven,
because, these aren't just any chocolate biscuits,
- these are Marks and Spencers chocolate biscuits!
Through the window I see the little boy who shot me
with his fingers minutes earlier.
To show him there are no hard feelings,
I give him a chocolate biscuit
- a taste of heaven.

# Sellotape

Why can I never find
the end of the sellotape?
Why do I wait and wait
trying to find the see-through line,
turning the roll, round and round
like a hamster wheel revolving
in a hamster cage?
The end of the tape
always manages to escape!
Holding the roll next to my nose,
looking like a seal with a ball
- except wearing clothes.
Scratching at the plastic
with my nail, doomed to fail
trying to find
an invisible line.
Turning the roll, time after time
only to find it's on the run.
End of sellotape
what have you done?
Why do you hide,
what is your crime?
You are a master of disguise,
give yourself up
surrender to the present
that needs wrapping!

I promise I'll cut you neatly with scissors,
no snapping.
They can put a man on the moon,
they can put a picture of the Mona Lisa
on a single grain of rice.
They can even make school dinners that taste nice!
But, finding the end of the sellotape
is like looking for a crumb in a cake.

# Seeing A Kingfisher Bird

Flying low,
weaving between the sunken shopping trolleys
and half-submerged washing machines
- whose whiter than white dreams
are long since gone.
Looking for its breakfast,
the stealth bomber of the bird world.
Who isn't hungry when the day begins?
Weaving above the polluted, rubbish filled canal.
What could live here?
What would want to live here?
But since when did nature ever ask why.
Electric blue wings shatter the icy London winter sky,
beat away the capital's greyness
in a spectrum between green and violet,
cutting across the tower block emptiness.
The London winter swept temporarily out of business.
Suddenly gone
but the memory flies on.

# My Daughter's Foot

Five soft little sleeping toes
Peeping out from beneath a warm duvet
like tiny tortoise heads
looking out from under a cotton shell.
Not yet ready to face the cold morning.
Having petite Burrito's dreams of nail varnish,
should they go,
pink, purple  or peach,
or better still,
just rainbow.
I give them a tickle
they start to giggle and wriggle.

# Music Fits Your Ears Like Your Socks Fit Your Toes

We didn't make music,
- it made us.
Beginning inside our mother.
Her heartbeat was the rhythm of love.
We didn't find music,
- it found us.
Followed directions to our ears
then played along with our hopes dreams and fears.
We don't hold music,
- it holds us.
Words and sounds that reach down
into your soul,
lifting you high above, help life be understood.
Music, makes you leave your seat,
makes your bones dance with your feet,
makes us sing the words we speak,
brings us together, cheek to cheek.
Music is sound's heartbeat.

# A Brush With Freedom

I am trying to brush our little girl's hair,
- she won't allow it!
Refusing to let me or the brush get near,
she growls and bares her teeth at me.
Now, she is hiding under the table like an escaped rabbit,
hopping around the living room floor.
I hop after her like a big kangaroo waving a brush.
At the height of the chase she suddenly stops and says
'If you'll eat imaginary kangaroo leaves, I'll let you brush
my hair.'
Both of us start to eat big handfuls of invisible leaves.
'Now, can I comb your hair?' I ask.
'No!' she says, 'I'll do it myself, give me the brush!'
I hand her the brush, she hops over to the window,
looks at her reflection in the glass,
then throws the brush out of the window.
She looks at me again and says,
'Where did all these kangaroo leaves come from?'

# Rain

Makes windscreen wipers start to dance.
Little children try and catch it on their tongues.
Leaves watery mirrors on the pavement.
Colours a blue sky grey.
Turns a picnic into a panic.
Persuades grown ups to play
'Hide 'n' Seek' in doorways.
Puts wellington boots on your feet.
Tickles the flowers out of the ground.
Hangs out together on windows.
Laughs as it races down drains and pipes.
Glues clothes to skin.
Made Gene Kelly start singing and dancing.
Marries the sun and has a rainbow child.
Fills the street with marching umbrellas.
Plays the drums on the roofs of houses.
Ruins your hair,
- especially mine.

# Dolly Sleepover

Early morning
sleep walking
towards Cornflakes
and a waterfall of milk.
Putting on my slippers,
my furry toe caves.
The first feels warm, cosy and fleecy.
It feels good like a slipper should.
The second feels different.
The second feels invaded.
Something hard and pointy is in there.
Three Polly Pocket dolls
are tucked up under a piece of white tissue.
They are sleeping in a line
having Polly Pocket dreams
of all the little shoes they have lost.
Wakey wakey, Pollys!
Time to face the world!
Time to think dresses and outfits,
and eat cotton wool for breakfast
served on a bottle-top plate.
Come on Pollys, don't be late!

# The Moon

The moon is like a mysterious belly button
filling up with the fluff of heaven.
The moon is like a lonely biscuit
being dunked in the tea of the night.
The moon is like a magical bath plug
stopping the darkness from swirling away.
The moon is like a silver pizza
being delivered to the angels.
The moon is like a glowing bride's dress
walking down the aisle of the galaxy.
The moon is like a far away cornflake
in the breakfast bowl of universe.
The moon is like a giant nostril
sniffing the cosmos.
The moon is like a golden football
in the World Cup of the stars.

# At The Bottom Of The Sandpit

At the bottom of the sandpit you will find:
some sand,
buckets and spades,
a couple of buried parents,
A sign saying 'Put Sand Here',
lots of homework,
a Thomas The Tank Engine,
- that became a Thomas the sank engine.
A Luis Vuitton designer handbag,
- that is now just a sandbag.
All the lost secrets of ancient Egypt,
if that is where the sand came from.
If, the sand came from Bournemouth,
all the lost secrets of ancient Bournemouth.
A witch,
(yes, a sand-witch, and her cat called Crust).
A little supermarket that only sells sand
called Sandsburys.
A small child that liked sand so much,
they decided to stay down there digging to Australia.

# The Magic Of The New Year

It was New Year's Eve,
a special and magical time.
In the streets people danced,
on the corners musicians played.
On top of a table
was a lady.
She was a belly dancer,
dancing for the New Year,
a special and magical time.
Her belly was moving round and round
like a little washing machine,
spinning away.
In her belly button
shone a red diamond,
bright red as a traffic light
shining under the street lamps.
She started to go faster and faster,
the diamond spinning round and round,
her belly stretching like an elastic band,
going faster and faster,
spinning like a frisbee,
until the diamond flew out and landed
in a man's drink.
The man drank the drink.
He drank the belly diamond.
He spluttered, then he coughed
the belly diamond back out.
The belly diamond flew from between his lips
and landed back in the dancer's belly button.
It was New Year's Eve,
a special and magical time.

# Two Types Of Parents

There are two types of parents.
Parents who care;
they wake you up in the morning
with milk and cookies,
singing to you softly
and carry you down the stairs.
They warm your slippers up for you in the oven
and give you ice cream on Pizza for breakfast.
They take you to school in a helicopter,
then stand outside your classroom window,
holding up a big sign that says
'We love you'.
The other kind of parents,
are the ones who
couldn't care less;
they wake you up by
putting rats in your bed.
They slide you down the stairs on a toothbrush.
For breakfast they give you your slippers to eat...
Cold!
They roll you to school in a dustbin,
and when you're at school they move house!
Thankfully, most of us have parents
who are a bit of both.

# Keys

Keys are silver,
keys are gold,
keys are something
you can hold.

Keys get jingled,
keys get jangled,
keys make music
when they're handled.

Keys in history,
keys full of mystery.
Sometimes keys
can be very risky (ris-key).

Keys lock drawers,
keys open doors,
Keys are silver laws
that **K**eep **E**verything **Y**our**S**.

Keys are lost,
keys are found,
keys are something
that go ... in your pocket.

# My Mate Darren

When I was a kid, my best mate Darren had
a great way of getting his toy soldiers to have a war.
He'd line them up on the kitchen floor,
close the kitchen door, draw the kitchen window blind,
set an alarm clock to ring in one minute's time,
switch off the kitchen light, making the kitchen dark as
night.
Then he'd take his tennis racquet
and swing it from left to right with all his might,
knocking his soldiers everywhere,
sending them flying through the air.
Making them spin - even his dog joined in,
scampering about with a mouthful of toy soldiers sticking
out.
Then, when the alarm clock would ring, whichever side
had the most soldiers still standing would win.
Years later, Darren now a man, strong and big,
was helping his mum bring in a brand new fridge.
When he moved the old one,
he found underneath, in the dirt and the grease
three toy soldiers who were still fighting the war,
waiting for an enemy that wasn't there anymore.
He dusted them down, stood them gently on the ground
and with as much love as he could,
he told them,
'It's over, you no longer need to be a toy soldier.

You can go back to your wives,
your families and friends you used to know,
lead your former lives ... the fighting finished
10 years ago.'
As gently as he could, he told them,
'There is no more war.'
- But, no one told his dog,
who ran back in and chewed them up once more.

# How High

How high would you climb,
if you could not fall?
How far would you go,
if you could go anywhere at all?
What questions would you ask,
if you always got an answer?
What moves would you make,
if 'Strictly Come Dancing' made you a dancer?
What pictures would you paint,
if you had a brush?
What songs would you sing,
if everyone listened with a hush?
What stories would you tell
if someone always heard?
How much more would you soar,
if you had wings like a bird.

# Toast

My little girl woke up
and she wanted toast,
so we went to the kitchen.
Which, is the home of toast,
the place where toast lives.
I mean, when you want toast
you don't go to the library
or to the petrol station!
Or to the shoe shop!
It's to the kitchen - the 'Land of Toast'.
I made her some toast.
She carried it using both hands,
holding them out like she was
carrying a royal crown for a queen.
Taking little steps, heel to toe
- as if walking on a rope across a waterfall -
she went into the living room
to sit on the sofa, to eat her toast
whilst watching 'CBeebies'.
I made myself some toast, carried it into the living room,
to also sit on the sofa
and to also watch 'CBeebies'.
But, when I entered the living room
she was not sat on the sofa,
she was next to the television,
trying to put her toast into the BlueRay DVD player.
When I asked her why,
she said, 'It's because I want to watch
'Toast', the movie!'

# I Saw God

He was sitting on a cloud,
he was laughing very loud.
An angel had told him a joke
And now he was laughing so much
he couldn't speak.
I said, 'What's so funny?'
But, this just made him laugh even more.
He laughed so hard
he started to fall through his cloud.
Bits of cloud caught in his beard,
making him look a bit weird.
He even had cloud in his hair
- his hair was getting funky up there!
Then, the cloud started to laugh
- jokes spread like that.
So, I asked again,
'What's so funny?'
An angel that couldn't laugh any more said,
'Life's more fun with a smile'.

# The Inflatable Boy

The inflatable boy awoke,
jumped out of his inflatable bed,
ran his inflatable comb
over his inflatable head.
Ran down the inflatable stairs,
sat in one of the inflatable chairs,
Ate his inflatable toast – yum, yum -
cooked for him by his
inflatable mum.
Brushed his inflatable teeth.
put his inflatable shoes
on his inflatable feet.
Then, he ran down the inflatable street.
But, he was no inflatable fool,
he was on his way to his inflatable school.
As he ran he saw something shiny and thin,
a very hard, silver and pointed thing -
It was a pin. Something new to him!
What could it be, what was it for?
He was in awe, he wanted to explore!
Just what was this?
He stuck it in his finger, which started to hiss.
There was no time for waiting,
the inflatable boy was deflating.
As fast as could, he ran to school,
entered the gate - too late!

Right then and there
his legs ran out of air.
He started to fall,
accidentally sticking the pin into the school wall.
The whole school started to hiss.
Hearing this,
out ran the head teacher, as the school began to shrink.
The head teacher didn't know what to think.
He yelled, 'Give me the pin!'
Fumbling, the inflatable boy accidentally stuck it in him!
The head teacher started to hiss,
and as he slowly crumpled to the ground
he told the inflatable boy,
'Not only have you let yourself down,
you've let me down,
and worst of all you've let the whole school down!'

# I've Got A Dog That Draws

I've got a dog, it's not like yours,
because my dog draws.
Your dog knows how to fetch,
my dog knows how to sketch.
Your dog likes to bury a bone,
my dog likes to mix shade and tone.
Your dog likes to wag its tail,
my dog likes to get things to scale.
Some dogs like to give each other
a good sniffin',
my dog would rather enter
a painting competition.
Your dog can roll over,
my dog can use Crayola.
Your dog likes to bark,
my dog likes to make great art.
Some dogs like to lick yer',
my dog can draw the perfect picture.

# The Rugby Pillow

One day at school we played rugby
for the first time ever.
None of us had played before,
nobody knew what was going on.
And to make it even harder,
we had to use a pillow
because the school didn't have a rugby ball.
It was strange, everybody started acting like they were
getting ready for bed.
As soon as some people caught the pillow
they started sitting on it.
A few actually tried to go to sleep.
My mate Darren said his house was just across the road
and he could get a duvet and an alarm clock,
if this was any help?
We all found it incredibly hard to run with the pillow,
but Darren - who could move like the wind -
stuffed the pillow up his shirt
and set off like a pregnant rocket.
'Tackle him, tackle him!'
yelled Mr Garner, our games teacher.
'We can't, Sir', we said, 'he's having a baby.'
At that, Mr Garner,
who thought he was quite trendy and cool,
(because he drove a Toyota) shot off
to try and catch Darren.
But Darren - who could move like the wind -
just kept on going, straight through the rugby posts
and onwards to the school gates.
'Where are you going?' yelled a tiring Mr Garner.
'To the hospital, to have my baby, Sir.'

# What If

What if the sky was green and the grass was blue?
What if you were me and I was you?
What if you turned on the tap and a hand came out?
What if giant toddlers moved the world about?
What if a teacher was afraid of knowledge?
What if my mum was an invisible burrito?
What if people were born old and grew younger
and younger until they finished up as little babies?
What if a book didn't have pages?
What if you could make time move slow or fast,
making the bad times go quick
and the good times last?
What if politicians never told lies?
What if you had fried eggs for eyes?
What if I stood like this for 20 minutes?
What if babies were born nine at a time?
What if everyone of us
Did one thing each day to put a smile on the world's face
Wouldn't that make where you live a better place?

# Flashback In Winter Light

One winter just before night,
snow fell so hard it flashed our bit of the world white.
The flakes fell so fast, school sent us home early from
class.
As we made our escape from things to be learnt,
we passed the factory gates where they made powdered
paints.
One of the delivery lorries had crashed, and
the powder paint it was carrying had splashed
coloured dust
of blue, silver, red and gold, onto the white falling cold.
The powder paint, which had made its escape,
embraced the snow crystals to form a new fate.
Water and powder flowed, making rainbow snow.
We scooped this up, taking it back to our yard.
Where we packed it hard,
till walls of coloured flake began to take shape.
Until an ice house of blue, silver, red and gold
shimmered in the cold.
We asked our mum if we could sleep in it that night,
and to our delight, she said, 'Alright.'
The night was bitter, but inside the rainbow snow house
everything was aglitter.

As we lay down to sleep, out of the dark
came a terrifying noise, rumbling deep.

The sound of the paint factory's machinery creak.
A low growling mix of rattling cries, which brought fear to our young eyes.
A grinding noise getting clearer,
angry machinery getting nearer.
We were seized by fear, it was like a dream.
Until I heard my little sister scream,
'It's the paint factory wanting back its dust!'
At that we leapt up and burst through the coloured ice,
driven on by a love for life.
Not stopping, until we were safe in our beds,
and sleep had melted the vengeful paint factory from our heads.
In the morning, we went back to see the house made of rainbow snow.
Under the sun, its walls still shone, but every bit of the colour was gone.
In the distance, the towering paint factory blew its whistle and looked on.

# Rock, Paper, Scissors

I'm waiting, waiting to appear at an assembly.
A little girl beside me is waiting.
She says 'While we're waiting,
would you like to play a game?'
I say 'Ok.'
She says, 'Let's play 'Rock, Paper, Scissors'.
I go, 'ROCK!'
She goes, 'Worm, wriggly worm, comes along
and munches up all your rock, eats every piece,
and you lose!'
'Ok,' I say, 'Let's play 'Rock, Paper, Scissors'.
I go, 'Scissors! - scissors will get her worm!
She goes, 'Two wriggly worms, they eat your scissors,
one at each end, munching them until there is none left,
and you lose!'
'Ok,' I say, 'Let's play 'Rock, Paper, Scissors'.
I go, 'Paper! - In fact a big piece of card
to wrap up worm-girls worms, fold into an envelope and
post those worms to South America!'
She goes, 'Lots of worms, wriggling from everywhere,
all over your paper, munching it up till there is none left,
and you lose!'
'Ok, let's play one more time. So worm-girl, made
entirely of worms, I'm going to get every one of them this
time!
Rock, Paper, Scissors!'
I go, 'Giant eagle: with huge wings, sharp beak, giant
talons, cawing fiercely!'
She goes, 'Don't be stupid, there are no giant eagles in
Rock, Paper, Scissors!'

# Playing Dare With The Waves

Above us is a sky coloured in by a child
with a new set of felt-tip pens.
Sand castles await their watery end -
by tide or toddler.
Location, location, location!
Golden grains guard the sun's trapped heat,
forcing bare feet
to dance and race across the fired surface.
By the edge of the sea,
a little girl plays 'dare' with the waves,
challenging the rolling water to wet her toes.
Her laughter re-mixes in with the sound of water
breaking.
Across the beach, a stranded newspaper wriggles its pages,
like a black and white crab on its back.
Flickering us glimpses of recessions, torrential back-home
rain
and soaring petrol prices.
But, here the issues are which flavour choc-ices?
Time and time again the girl edges forward,
to be pushed backwards up the beach by the chasing
ocean.
Her little feet
pedalling the shingle like a drummer brushing a cymbal.
White wave tips come after her in eager pursuit,
making her flick in reverse.
Eventually, she grows physically tired of this game.
Her desire for the contest is replaced by the need
For a 'Hello Kitty' ice-cream.
But, the ocean will never grow tired of this game
and tomorrow it will be waiting for her again.

# It's A New World Each Day

Choose the hour, choose the day,
choose the words you'll shape and say.
Choose the way sunlight cuts through trees,
electrifying dew-laced cobwebs,
that dance to the rhythm of the breeze.
Choose the shape of snowflakes,
choose a journey you cannot measure,
choose to unbury buried treasure.
Choose to share your choices,
choose to share different voices.
Choose time flying fast,
gone in the blink of an eye.
Choose making it last forever,
a minute that never ever says goodbye.
Choose to let your thoughts
float up and go beyond,
choose to believe that magic
leaps from the tip of a wand.
Choose to dream your own dreams,
choose to see everything
is not as it seems.
We all make choices, it's true,
make sure one of them
is to choose to be you.

# The Simpsons

(said in the theme tune of the show)

Marge, has got blue hair
and it goes up to there!
Bart's, bad from the start,
but he's got a good heart.
Lisa's, so smart, and she loves
to play her saxophone, all on her own.
Homer, is so slow,
and he always goes 'DOH!'
Maggie's, so sweet,
and you never see her feet.
They've all got lovely yellow skin,
and a finger missing.
Homer, has bad luck,
but loves a doughnut -
'HHMMMM DOUGHNUTAAARRRRGGG!'
In each show there's always a catchphrase we know.
Homer goes - 'DOH!'
Marge makes a sound like - 'Mmrrrrhhhhhhh'.
Bart says - 'EAT MY SHORTS' and 'NO PROBLEMO'.
Maggie goes - 'SUCK SUCK'.
And then, before you know it's over too soon - but
there's just time for LISA to say,
'IF ANYBODY WANTS ME I'LL BE IN MY ROOM!'

# A Day In The Life Of
# A One Pound Coin

Lena wakes, another school day breaks.
Down the stairs - five at a time, she skates.
Never hesitates, eats her cornflakes.
Can't be late, but also then her bed she makes,
and she even clears the table of the plates.
Seeing this, her mum puts her hand in her pocket,
and gives Lena a shiny one pound coin,
which Lena with a 'cor, thanks! ' - takes.
In the schoolyard everyone's chasing.
Lena sees Jason, She owes this kid a quid.
She pays him back, 'cos life's like that.
Jason's got that brand new coin in a spin,
tails never fails - heads we win.
The captains call the toss, the schoolyard
football match kicks off.
Jason's turn between the jumpers.
He's keeping out shot after shot,
I mean, saving some real thumpers!
Jason's flying through the sky,
he doesn't know it ,
he never even had a chance to say good bye.
Out of his pocket falls his shiny cash,
lost in the make believe 'Wembley' grass.

Sasha's not into football, she prefers a book.
She'd like to play it, but all the boys
say she too rough - as girls go, she's Power Puff.
She sees something shine in the grass.
She doesn't have to ask, she recognises that flash.
What luck - her hand goes down with a whisk and
she's picked up that glinting golden disc.
Home-time bell, run like hell. Sasha's on the bus,
pays her fare.
This kid says goodbye to her new  found
shiny quid, which is now being rattled around,
as the bus roars around town.
The bus stops and on hops Lena's mum.
She pays the driver with a fiver.
A shiny quid in her change,
as the bus pulls away with a roar.
And now she's walking in her front door -
'Pocket money day!' cries Lena.
Same one pound coin,
back in action once more.

# Children Of The Sun

Why are there so many children of different colour
and shape,
here, there and everywhere all over the place?
It is because of something long ago,
when the sky was first made and the sun first began
to glow.
In fact, all of the world was made by the sun,
because everything needs heat and light to become.
And, when it was all done;
complete with rivers, trees, mountains and seas
and a cooling breeze,
the sun sent into the world a girl and a boy
to enjoy every day and sunrise.
But, eventually, they got tired of just hearing
their own happy cries and the life they led,
so they decided to mix water, flour, milk and egg
and make their own little children out of bread.
They mixed the mix and shaped the dough,
until there were six bread children that were ready to
bake slow.
And when they were cooked, the boy and girl
took them in their hands, breathed
life into them, and said, 'Welcome to our lands.'
The little bread children were such a delight,
the boy and girl said, 'Let's make some more tonight!'

Last time, they made six, but this time
they only made four, so these ones were slightly
bigger than the ones they made before.
They meant to bake them through,
but like most children they couldn't wait
to see what they would do.
So, they plucked them out of the oven
only half-cooked, and these ones a little lighter looked.
Again and again, they made more,
each a little different than the ones before -
they baked them short,  they baked them long -
and breathed life into each and every one.
The most important part of all this
was to give them love with a little kiss.
So, the little bread children grew up loving and good
and were of many different shades of colour and size.
Then to the boy and girl's surprise, the little bread
children went their own way, to live around the world,
to work and play.
And that is why
you and me
are this way today.

# The Gift Of Now

Have you ever wondered
why chocolate tastes so good?
Have you ever wondered
what it must be like not to be loved?
Have you ever wondered
why everything can't be understood?
And have you ever wondered
what Little Red Riding Hood
would have been called, if she hadn't
worn a hood?
Have you ever wondered
where you are when you're asleep?
Have you ever wondered
why feelings go so deep?
Have you ever wondered
why you keep the things you keep?
And have you ever wondered
Why school dinners taste like smelly feet?
Have you ever wondered
where you'll be in ten years time?
Have you ever wondered
why we like our poetry to have imagination,
a story and well thought out rhyme?
Have you ever wondered
how you fit everything in your mind?

Have you ever wondered
what it must be like to be
the back end of a cow, in a pantomime?
Have you ever wondered
why time goes so fast?
Have you ever wondered why everything cannot
last?
Have you ever wondered
how you'll make your own children laugh?
And, have you ever wondered
What it must be like to
slide down the neck of a Giraffe!

# McBroccoli

Imagine if McDonalds only did Broccoli?
You could go in and order
a Big McBroccoli Whopper,
or a McBroccoli Nugget Happy Meal
and a Fillet of Broccoli Sandwich.
While for breakfast,
there'd be a Broccoli McMuffin.
To wash it all down,
an ice cold delicious Broccoli shake.
And all served
with a side order of Brussels Sprouts.
HHHHMMMM, succulent pieces of Broccoli,
crisp tasty sproutyness.
And the toys
would be plastic bits of Broccoli.
And if you were really lucky,
you might walk into
one of their 'restaurants'
and meet their world famous clown
'Roccoli McBroccoli'.

# Lionel and Rosie
## Two Really Useful Cats

One day Lionel got my daughter dressed,
- me and her mum were most impressed.
A bit later Rosie took her to school
- all the teachers said, 'That's pretty cool!'
A bit later, Lionel did the cooking,
- that was when none of us was looking.
Afterwards, Rosie did the dishes,
- we thought, 'She's only looking for fishes.'
Finally, Lionel made a cappuccino coffee,
that had perfect froth
- But we said, 'He's only showing off.'
Then Lionel and Rosie said, 'Enough's enough,
from now on, we're only gonna do cat stuff!'

# Buying Books

Too babyish – too long –
too short – too pricey –  too scary
too girly – too many monsters and not enough fairies.

Too 'not me' – too hard –
too stupid – too many pictures
and too many witches!

Too many princesses, too many fishes,
too many kings
And not enough wishes.

Too many pages – too taking ages
too many for just one to be chosen –
too late -  the book shop's closing!

# You Can Do Amazing Stuff

I closed my eyes and the light was gone.
I opened my eyes and the light came back on.
I jumped in the air
and the ground wasn't there.
When I came back down
so did the ground.
I span round and round
and the world started to spin.
When I stopped and stood still
the world wasn't moving.
I remembered a tropical beach that was far away.
My memory took me back to that beach
and I stayed on that beach for rest of the day.

# Baby Within

Baby within,
just beneath
your mother's skin.
In a womb,
coming out soon.
Gift from above,
made of love.
Like belly button fluff,
somehow you are made -
grow, don't fade.

# Home Is

Home is a sofa that's always waiting for your bottom!
Home is finding something down the back of it you had
forgotten.
Home is sitting on the stairs pretending to be a mountain
climber.
Home is a place where someone rescues you from a
spider.
Home is sometimes untidy, messy and a disaster zone
catastrophe.
Home is making it look tidy for visitors who get treated
like a VIP.
Home is getting squashed between grown ups on that
sofa
because they refuse to move over.
Home is arguing with your brother and sister
Home is feeling so close to them it's like a never ending
game of Twister!
Home is your Dad pretending to be Elvis.
Home is your Mum pretending to be Lady Gaga.
Home is you pretending to be Elvis Gaga.
Home is pictures of your family new and old.
Home is a place that stays with you wherever you go.
Home is the smell of burnt toast.
Home is a place that you love the most.
Home is not p£rf3ct ,
but it's always worth it.
Home is ten thousand hand-made memories.
Home is where your heart's treasure is.

# Underwater learning

If our teacher were a mermaid,
She'd fill the classroom up with water,
colourful tropical fish would swim under our desks
and nibble our toes.
At snack time we'd get seaweed biscuits
with Seahorse milk to drink!

If our teacher were a mermaid,
she'd stick real starfish in our books for good work,
at playtime we'd ride around on dolphins.
We'd go to museums in a submarine!
and stop off at Atlantis on the way back!

If our teacher were a mermaid
we'd take our homework home in a fishtank
learn to read pirate treasure maps
and how to walk the plank.
At the end of the day,
she'd open the window and swim away.

# My Gran

Every winter you knitted me a new woolly hat,
always slate grey, just like the East Yorkshire winter sky.
By the time I was fourteen,
I had several of these, each slightly larger than
the previous.
When you made bread, you saved me a fistful of dough,
so that I could make a bread man,
with currants for buttons and eyes.
Whenever my mum called me stupid
(usually because I was doing something stupid).
You reminded her that when she was my age
she was twice as stupid.
Telling of the time she came home without her shoes,
or had fallen down a coal heap.
It soon turned down the sound of her voice.
You still had a World War Two Anderson air raid shelter in
your back yard.
We'd sit in there, just the two of us,
you'd tell me about the nights the German planes came,
bombs whistling out of the sky,
the high pitched falling sound growing louder
as you waited for them to explode.
Whenever you picked me up from school
you were never late, I'd see your face peering into the
classroom,
soft eyes shining out from beneath a slate grey woolly
hat,

long before any other kid saw a face they wanted to see.
After school we made butter and sugar sandwiches;
I can still taste the sweetness today.
Even in your eighties, you still rode a bike.
Once I saw you racing through the town,
passing cars.
Someone shouted,
'Look at that old lady, she thinks she's in 'The Tour De France!'
But I just said,
'That's no old lady, that's my Gran'.

# Where Did Yesterday Go?

Vanished, into thin now.
A disappearing act like no other,
like Cinderella, running down the chimes of midnight.
The glass slipper smashes,
Everything that was here runs for cover.
Its fragments bejewel our memories.
Another twenty-four hours has evaporated,
Their perforated edges torn away.
Lonely universes are poetic.
Goodbye yesterday –
what have you become?
A puzzle of recollection and remembrances.
Meetings, journeys and coincidences,
Pieces that loosely fit together...
embers of flames that burned,
ashes that are raked over.
Sights, sounds and colours still so vivid.
But now turned to postcards...
written in ink that smoulders and smudges.
Wish you were here,
so far so near.
Hand delivered with love.
Written in hope.
Now a new hand is dealt.
The same new cards from a familiar deck.

Meaning, meetings, mistakes and domestic earthquakes
dealt at random
destined to reshuffle and re-land.
Similar in value and worth,
just another twenty-four hours on Earth.

# I Want To Be A Teacher

I want to be a teacher
and teach and teach and teach.
I want to be a teacher
and speak that teacher speak!

Put up your hand.
Does everyone understand?
No talking, no rushing,
no running just walking, no pushing.

I want to be a teacher
and teach and teach and teach.
I want to be a teacher
and speak that teacher speak!

Remember your finger-spaces.
Fasten your shoelaces.
It was fun in the stone ages,
this classroom is a learning oasis.

I want to be a teacher
and teach and teach and teach.
I want to be a teacher
and speak that teacher speak!

The Vikings, they were scary.
The Vikings, they were hairy.
The Vikings, were military,
you'd never find them in a library.

I want to be a teacher
and teach and teach and teach.
I want to be a teacher
and speak that teacher speak!

Today we are going to grow.
Today we are going to know.
Today we are the star of the show
and at 3.15 we are going to go!

# The Mighty Yorkshire Pudding

It's more than just a pudding.
Have you really been looking?
It's a volcano filled with lava gravy
or a harbour for a broccoli navy.
Wembley Stadium, for two teams to run about
except instead of a football, it's a sprout!
An impenetrable golden crispy castle
where beans and carrots battle.
A space craft from a far away distant galaxy
driven by evil alien celery.
A gravy bank to be robbed of its loot
by hard boiled bandit beetroot.
It's Hogwarts and that carrot in the middle is
Herbmione Granger
Here comes Harry Pottertato to save her from Volderfork
danger.
If your mum and dad tell you not to play with your food,
tell them to not do so would be cruel and rude
because all these vegetable animals need saving.
The plate is flooding!
All aboard Noah's Ark,
The HMS Yorkshire pudding.

# Parents

Aren't happy that
they never get any sleep.
Aren't happy that
you've broken the things they wanted to keep.
Aren't  happy that
you make them run about.
Aren't happy that
their hair is falling out.
Aren't happy that
you continuously ask 'Are we nearly there yet'?
Aren't happy that
they had to go all the way back home -
to collect the  thing you weren't supposed to forget!
Aren't happy that
they have to clean up all of the time.
Aren't happy that
kids love playing with slime.
Aren't happy that
The P has fallen off
Their **P**arent' sign.

# Matilda

There was a girl called Matilda.
She could fix mean people like Bob the builder.
She sorted out her stupid parents,
by giving them both their deserved deterrents!
But of all her problems, her head teacher was the worst!
The Trunch made every kids life cursed.
So Matilda taught her a lesson,
using magic and determination as her weapon.
Now, The Trunch didn't go back to her mother,
instead, she's taking part on Celebrity Big Brother.

# We Had That Michael Rosen
# In My Car

We had that Michael Rosen in my car.
We weren't going far.
He never stopped talking,
next time he's walking.

# We Are Words

Their meaning, their dreaming,
The message they're streaming.
We use them to shape our lives, as bribes
to make enemies and allies.
We use them to find our tribes.
We are words,
their story, their song.
They define right and wrong,
always on the tip of your tongue.
We pin them to the page,
we read them to be amazed.
We are words,
they connect us, correct us.
make us find one another.
Yes, they collect us.
Ashes to ashes, dust to dust,
A lie, a promise, a trust.
We are words,
We dance with them through time,
They are our partners in rhyme
Cool, cruel or kind,
The stitching in our story-line
The eloquent ties that bind.

Poet in residence for the **ROALD DAHL** Museum 2013/2014 & Star of BBC2's/CBBC's **'Big Slam Poetry House'**. His poetry is funny and moving and his poetry workshops produce extraordinary poems from children of all ages. Paul has been poet in residence at 10 Secondary Schools and 14 Primary Schools. Paul was Poet for the London Borough of Brent (London's 5th coolest Borough) and he performed at the new **Wembley Stadium**. He has 2 poems in the **New 09 Penguin's A-Z** of Childrens poetry. Paul has also performed at 10 Edinburgh festivals, 1 Eton College, **5 Glastonbury's** and on a 73 Bus, which made the and finally...bit of the 6pm national news. Paul has worked and performed with **Michael Rosen**, George Best, **Miranda Hart**, Will Self, John Hegley, Benjamin Zepphaniah, Andrea Leavy & Rastamouse to name but a few. Paul was one of the **London 2012 Olympic** 'Shake the Dust' Poets & 2012 Smile London Poets. In 2013 Paul was Poet for the London Borough of Islington's 2013 Word Festival and Worked with **Arsenal Football club** (Yes that one) performing his poetry in their dressing room and on their pitch!

**www.paul-lyalls.uk**


'With 100 Year 5 children, you certainly inspired and injected enthusiasm both for the children & the staff ... you allowed quirky and fun moments of their lives to be captured and it was something that children of all abilities could connect and spark from. We all loved re-reading our poems.'

*Head of year Danes Hill School.*


Edited by Cordelia De Peon